Cairo, C and Chaos

By Alicia Klepeis
Illustrated by Simon Abbott

Rourke
Educational Media
rourkeeducationalmedia.com

www.rourkeeducationalmedia.com

Edited by: Keli Sipperley
Cover and Interior layout by: Renee Brady
Cover and Interior Illustrations by: Simon Abbott

Library of Congress PCN Data

Cairo, Camels, and Chaos / Alicia Klepeis
 (Rourke's World Adventure Chapter Books)
 ISBN (hard cover)(alk. paper) 978-1-63430-397-2
 ISBN (soft cover) 978-1-63430-497-9
 ISBN (e-Book) 978-1-63430-591-4
 Library of Congress Control Number: 2015933797

Printed in the United States of America, North Mankato, Minnesota

Dear Parents and Teachers:

Rourke's Adventure Chapter Books engage readers immediately by grabbing their attention with exciting plots and adventurous characters.

Our Adventure Chapter Books offer longer, more complex sentences and chapters. With minimal illustrations, readers must rely on the descriptive text to understand the setting, characters, and plot of the book. Each book contains several detailed episodes all centered on a single plot that will challenge the reader.

Each adventure book dives into a country. Readers are not only invited to tag along for the adventure but will encounter the most memorable monuments and places, culture, and history. As the characters venture throughout the country, they address topics of family, friendship, and growing up in a way that the reader can relate to.

Whether readers are reading the books independently or you are reading with them, engaging with them after they have read the book is still important. We've included several activities at the end of each book to make this both fun and educational.

Are you ready for this adventure?

Enjoy,
Rourke Educational Media

Table of Contents

Chapter One

A Surprise Assignment

"Can you shush it, Samal?" It was Anara's day to sit in the front seat for the ten-minute drive home from school. But her twin Samal was already launching into a re-cap of the day's events in her fifth grade classroom, even before she'd buckled her seat belt.

The rule was that whichever girl sat up front got to talk about her day first. And 7-year-old Oliver was begging for a stop at Nonna's Bakery. The noise level was at a 9.5 out of 10–and they hadn't even left the school parking lot yet. Not that there was anything unusual about this chaos. The short ride home was one of the best times to share news from the day since Mom headed into her office once everyone had a snack.

"Sorry, Ollie. I can't stop at Nonna's today. I have a conference call in an hour that I have to get ready for. Maybe on Friday, okay?" Mom looked at Ollie in the rearview mirror. He was pouting, but would likely get over it once he found something appealing in the pantry.

"Mom, did I tell you about the math test I have next week in Mrs. Hanson's class? It's going to be a killer." Anara was not a math person.

Just then, Mom's cell phone rang. Anara answered it. "Yes, she's here but she's driving. Can I take a message?" She scribbled notes down on the pad Mom kept on the dashboard.

Samal asked, "Who was that? You were making such a weird face."

"Yeah, well don't forget, my face is your face," Anara retorted. Anara and Samal were identical twins so whenever one of them criticized the other's looks, that was their favorite comeback.

Anara looked at Mom. "It was some guy named Dr. Williamson from UNESCO. He asked you to call him back as soon as possible."

Mom sighed. "Thanks, babe. I'll call him back when we get home." Mom worked for UNESCO, the United Nations Educational, Scientific and

Cultural Organization. The agency was part of the UN. Mom's job involved making sure different cultural and natural sites around the world were maintained properly.

Once they'd parked, Anara, Samal, and Oliver flew up the three flights of stairs to their two-bedroom apartment. It was crammed but cozy. It never took long for the feeding frenzy to begin. Practically every day it was the same scene: Ollie curled up on the couch with a bag of pretzels; Samal had a huge bowl of cereal with almond milk; and Anara made herself a vanilla milkshake and peanut butter toast.

After they ate, the twins watched their favorite cooking show. They were addicted to the Food Network. Ollie, the history buff, was playing a game on Mom's iPad. When Mom came out from her study looking totally frazzled, none of the kids even noticed.

"Guys?" Silence. "GUYS!" Mom was not a yeller, so everyone knew something was up when she raised her voice.

Anara paused the show and Ollie took his

headphones off. "Yes, Mom?"

"Let's sit at the kitchen table, please. I am freaking out a little bit. Samal, would you put the kettle on? I could use a cup of chamomile tea."

The kids quickly joined Mom at the small round table in front of the window. "So here's the story. Dr. Williamson called because the leader of the UNESCO team that was heading to Egypt next week needs emergency surgery. He knows I regularly lead this type of team."

"Can't we just stay at Dad's like we usually do when you go away?" Ollie suggested.

Mom ruffled his hair. "I texted him and he has a conference that week. But Dr. Williamson really doesn't have another person who can go."

Anara suggested asking their grandmother Vovó. Mom said it was too late to call tonight since she lived in Helsinki, Finland, which is seven hours ahead of New York time.

The next afternoon, when the kids hopped into the car, Mom didn't look happy. "Vovó can't meet up with us," she said grimly. "She's traveling to London that week with a few friends from high school. I can't entertain you all day in Egypt while I'm working. I'm at my wit's end. What are we going to do?"

Chapter Two

Plan B and Passport Problems

It was Oliver who had the next brainwave. "Do you know anyone in Egypt, Mom?" he asked. Anara and Samal rolled their eyes at each other, believing it was a dumb question.

Thinking really hard, Mom scrunched up her face. "You know what, Ollie? I actually do know someone there. A suitemate of mine from college, Allison, lives in Cairo with her family. We keep in touch on Facebook now and then. You know how people always say, 'Let me know if you ever make it here'? I'll give it a try."

Mom disappeared into her office. A few minutes later, she came out smiling. "Allison happened to be online when I emailed her. She offered to host you guys while I work."

"What about school, Mom? The school year

Egypt Packing List:

Math sheets
Journals
Something to read or do on plane
(mazes, word searches,
sticker books)
Pens, colored pencils, markers
Sketchpad
Stuffed animals (Samal - rainbow
chameleon; Anara - elephant;
Oliver - buffalo)
Bathing suits and hats
Sneakers and sandals
Shorts and T-shirts
Underwear and socks
Pants
Pajamas

practically just started. There are no vacations in October. Can we really miss two or three weeks of classes?" Samal asked the questions but Anara was worried too.

It turned out that their teachers were actually excited about the trip. The twins' teachers assigned a few math worksheets and asked them to keep a journal. Oliver's teacher just said to have a good trip. That was the good part about being in second grade.

Anara and Samal researched October's weather in Cairo and Aswan. Oliver was psyched to hear it would be between 64 and 86 degrees, with virtually no rain. He loved warm weather.

"Hey girls," Ollie asked with a toothless smile, "Do you think there will be swimming pools anywhere we stay?" Anara grinned. She was like a fish in the water.

"I never even thought of that," Samal answered. "Let's surprise Mom and make a list of what we want to bring on the trip. She'll love it."

Over minestrone soup and garlic bread, Anara showed Mom the list. "Wow, you've definitely got the ball rolling, guys! I have some things to add but the list looks good. For one thing, you girls are not likely to wear shorts much because in the Islamic culture, young women tend to be covered up more."

Samal asked, "Are we going to be in dresses all the time? Do we have to wear headscarves?" As a fashionista, Samal didn't want her style to be cramped. She loved wearing crazy colors and funky outfits.

Mom giggled. "No, Samal, you don't have to completely change the way you dress. You just need to respect the culture and protect yourselves from the Sun."

******

In the chaos of getting ready to go, Mom became a nearly invisible blur. She was up late booking hotels, running into Manhattan to the UN offices, and doing zillions of errands.

After dinner one night, a shriek came from Mom's bedroom. Samal rushed in. "What's the matter? Are you having a heart attack?" Ever since she'd taken a first aid class, Samal worried about heart attacks.

Mom laughed. "No, love. My heart is fine...But Ollie's passport is expired."

The next day Oliver got to miss school to go to the New York Passport Agency on Hudson Street with Mom and Dad. Everyone breathed a sigh of relief when the call came that Ollie's expedited passport was ready to pick up – just two days before their departure date.

Dad dropped off guidebooks, magnetic games for Oliver, and magazines for the twins before heading to his conference in Atlanta. He also picked up an Arabic phrasebook since that was Egypt's official language. "Make sure you guys are good for your mom," Dad said. "This trip is a big deal. She really needs you all to be cooperative. I am so jealous that you're going to Egypt."

He hugged all the kids. Leaning in toward Mom, he said, "Sorry I can't help with this one, Jess. I hope you have a great trip. Email if there's anything I can do from this end."

"Thanks." Mom seemed grateful for the support. Even though they were divorced, they still tried to help each other. Anara and Samal were glad about that. Some of their classmates' parents were divorced and couldn't even attend school concerts without arguing.

All four Nylunds were relieved when they finally boarded Flight 4716 heading to Cairo International Airport. Oliver thought it was cool that all the announcements were in Arabic and English. On the flight, the girls watched a couple movies and several cooking shows. By the time everyone fell asleep, their brains were full of animation.

Chapter Three

Meeting the Mahfouz Family

~~~~~~

After their 12-hour flight, the twins were thrilled to touch down in Cairo. "I cannot wait to have some food," Anara announced. Samal agreed. The two of them were always hungry. After grabbing their bags at the carousel, they headed outside to the taxi stand. Mom's friend Allison advised against taking public transportation at night with all their bags.

Mom dug through her purse to find a printout of directions in Arabic to Allison's apartment. Allison's husband, Keb, emailed them before they left. When Mom handed the directions to the driver, he grinned. "Nice, New Cairo," he said, then loaded everyone's bags in the trunk.

Oliver pressed his face to the window for the entire 40-minute ride to Allison's place. He didn't want to miss anything. Gates blocked some of the neighborhoods they passed by, but Samal glimpsed what looked like mini-mansions through the bars. "Wow, these are some fancy houses! Do you think Allison and Keb live in a place like this?"

Mom laughed. "Since Allison is a teacher, probably not. But New Cairo is supposed to be quite nice. It's even slightly cooler than Cairo proper, partly because of its elevation."

"Was all of this desert before?" Oliver asked.

"It sure was, and not long ago. This development was planned in the early 2000s. It'll be fun to explore by daylight, won't it?"

The cab pulled up to a mustard-yellow building. It was about five or six stories high. The driver said "thank you" in English and patted Oliver on the head before departing. Mom pressed a buzzer labeled Mahfouz. A minute later, Allison and Keb came down and greeted them warmly.

Their apartment was on the fourth floor. It had several big windows. A crane was visible outside. "It's always good to go to bed early because the cranes and workers start shortly after dawn to beat the heat," Allison said. "You all look wiped

out. Just so you know, Jessica, you and Oliver will share Keb's study. And girls, you'll be in with our daughter, Rana. She's a pretty heavy sleeper so she's not likely to wake up when you go in. There's an air mattress for you in there."

"Allison, you forgot the most important thing - food!" Keb said, smiling. On the kitchen table was a mini-feast: *mahshi kurumb* (rice-and-meat-stuffed cabbage leaves), *tabbouleh* (bulgur wheat, parsley, and tomato with lemon juice and sesame seeds), lentil soup with bread, and a rice pudding with raisins and pistachios in it.

There was almost silence for a few minutes while they dove in. Since the Nylund kids lived in the diverse Queens borough of New York, they were always trying new foods – Pakistani, Lebanese, you name it. But Keb's cooking was divine. After stuffing their faces, Ollie and the twins were asleep in no time flat.

When the Sun rose early the next morning, Anara and Samal looked around. Rana was reading quietly in her bed. She smiled when she saw the twins were awake. Rana's room was decorated all in purple. It was amazing. Samal, a design fan, complimented her, "Wow! Your room is so cool, Rana!"

Rana beamed. "Thank you. My mom helped me decorate it. She was a design major in college." She looked at each of the twins. "I have to ask you, which of you is Anara and who's Samal?"

Samal answered, "I have a little scar in my left eyebrow." She pointed at it, "See? This is from when I tripped at the playground when I was two. And Anara often wears her hair in a bun."

Over a leisurely breakfast, Allison told the story of how she knew Mom from their days at Georgetown University in Washington, D.C. and how she met Keb at graduate school in New York. Ollie loved the breakfast mixture of eggs and fava beans. For a seven year old, he was often a more adventurous eater than his sisters. Mom gave Allison some hostess gifts – a big jug of New York State maple syrup, I Love NY t-shirts for all three of them, and a bag of American gum and candy.

When everyone was dressed, they went for a walk and explored the neighborhood. They passed by lots of shiny new apartment buildings. Keb explained that people who can afford to are flocking to New Cairo, with its many businesses and universities close by.

While Mom and Allison shopped at a local produce market for dinner ingredients, Keb took the four kids to a nearby park. He'd brought a soccer ball in his backpack. Without thinking, Anara and Samal took off their skirts since they had shorts underneath. Rana's mouth opened wide, though she said nothing. Keb also was quiet.

For a couple of minutes, the five of them kicked the ball around. Then a couple of older ladies walked by the field where they were playing. They got very close to the twins and started shouting in Arabic. They were pointing their fingers and scowling.

"What are they saying, Rana?" Anara asked.

"I'm not allowed to say those words – in English or in Arabic," Rana replied. Embarrassed, she looked down at her feet.

"Keb, what's the matter?" Samal queried.

"I didn't want to say anything, girls, because I

know what it's like to live in New York. But these elderly women are offended to see young ladies wearing shorts in public. It is considered very inappropriate, I'm afraid." Keb also looked like he'd like to sink into the ground below him.

"Oh my gosh, I totally forgot," Anara's face was scarlet. She quickly threw her skirt back on. "I'm so sorry, Keb." Samal got dressed fast too. The scorning women disappeared, but not without a last disapproving look at the twins.

"It's okay, girls. Don't let it get to you. Just try to remember in the future. Let's start again." The twins weren't sure about it. A small crowd had gathered nearby when they heard the ruckus. But it turned out that Keb was a bit of a neighborhood soccer celebrity. Some kids from the neighborhood joined in their pickup game. Keb acted as referee.

The rest of the day flew by. Rana and the twins listened to Egyptian pop music. Rana taught the girls how to tie a headscarf. She had lots of different headscarves and wore one every day. But Allison didn't since she wasn't Muslim. Oliver watched a soccer match on TV until it was time to enjoy their supper of spicy chickpea balls, called falafel, and chicken kebabs.

After dinner, Mom started packing for her 10-day business trip. Oliver became tearful. "I don't want you to go, Mom. I want to come with you," he said.

Mom tried to comfort him. She reminded him that he would meet other kids when Allison took him to school with her the next day. Allison worked at the International School of Cairo. Before bed, Anara and Samal asked Rana a million questions about what school was like. Rana answered some of them but was getting sleepy.

'You'll find out for yourselves tomorrow," Rana said. "Good night."

Chapter Four

Going to School in Egypt

Early the next morning, Mom headed to the train station. Anara thought it was strange that she was going to work on a Sunday. But Sunday was also a school day. Rana reminded her that Friday was the holy day for Muslims so students and workers typically had Friday and Saturday off each week.

"What should I wear to school, Allison?" Samal asked.

"Don't worry, Samal – we'll be able to get some secondhand uniforms at the school shop. You'll blend in with everyone else."

"Okay," Samal said. She was bummed out that she couldn't just wear one of her nice new skirts or pants.

After they arrived at school, the three Nylund kids got navy blue pants and simple white polo

shirts with the school logo embroidered on the front. Samal wasn't thrilled with the bland look but kept quiet.

As the art teacher, Allison knew all of the students. In every hallway, kids said, "Good morning, Mrs. Mahfouz."

Rana asked the twins, "Do you guys want to be in separate classrooms? That way you both can be a celebrity for a while."

Anara and Samal raised their eyebrows at each other. "Yes, please." They both liked the sound of that. "We are in different classrooms back home, too."

Samal went to Mrs. Halabi's class. Anara headed to Mrs. Kouri's room. Even from the classroom door, Anara thought she was going to like Mrs. Kouri. The door was covered in colorful posters of scenes from around the world and her classroom smelled faintly of vanilla.

Finally, Rana brought Oliver to Mrs. Toma's second grade classroom. She introduced Ollie to his buddy, a freckle-faced boy named Declan who recently moved to Cairo from England. Declan was so excited to be the expert at school after being the new kid last year. He showed Ollie the construction table full of Legos and the class pet, a chameleon named Jazzy.

Before they knew it, the Nylunds had gone through their whole first day of school. Over dinner, Allison asked them, "So what did you think about school in Egypt?"

"Everyone was so friendly!" Anara said. "There were kids in my class from Germany, Holland, Taiwan, Indonesia, and of course, Egypt. I really liked how Mrs. Kouri made geography such a fun class. We did some origami during our lesson on Japan. We don't even take geography back home."

"Mrs. Halabi's class was good too," Samal said. "An Egyptian girl named Reem was my buddy. She sat with me at lunch and introduced me to lots of kids. I even met a boy from Helsinki, near where our grandma Vovó lives. And in music I got to borrow a tambourine and join the orchestra."

Ollie was also excited to talk about his day. "I really liked using the math cubes. Declan's super good at math so he helped me with some problems

I didn't know how to do. And I learned how to play handball at recess. When I go home, I'm going to teach my friends."

"Wow, it sounds like things went well for all of you. I'm so glad. It's a great school." After clearing their plates, the Nylund kids wrote in their journals while Rana did a little homework.

The next few days flew by. The twins learned a bit of Arabic during the week. They practiced writing "hello" (ابحرم) and "goodbye" (ا عادو) in their journals. Ollie got into a regular morning soccer game with some of the other boys before the bell rang. And Samal became quite the handball player. A couple of nights Ollie was teary because Mom hadn't called much. But Keb would watch a bit of soccer on the TV with Oliver and then read him a bedtime story. It always made him feel better.

One night Dad called from Atlanta. Ollie and the girls told Dad that Allison and Keb taught them some Egyptian cooking. Dad made them promise to teach him on their next weekend in Brooklyn. Samal said she'd make Keb's recipe for baklava.

Anara offered to prepare a cucumber and chickpea salad.

On their last day at the International School of Cairo, the atmosphere at school was festive because the following week was vacation. Oliver, Samal, and Anara all exchanged addresses and emails with their new friends. Mrs. Kouri even brought in cupcakes as a little farewell celebration for Anara. At the school shop, Allison treated the three of them to pencil cases and pens with the school name and logo on them.

"Does anyone else feel like stopping to get an after school treat with me?" Allison asked.

Rana knew that this was an unusual opportunity. "Yes, please, Mum. Where are you thinking of going?" Anara, Samal, and Oliver were quiet in the back seat but smiling.

"Kenooz Siwa," Allison responded.

"No way! Really?" Clearly, this was an unusual choice from the excitement in Rana's voice.

A few minutes later, the four kids followed Allison into the fancy restaurant. The waiter led them to a low-set table in the back. They sat on puffy gold cushions. Colorful brass-and-glass lanterns glowed above them. "Wow," Samal said. "This is so fancy. I feel like I'm in a movie."

Rana said, "This is my favorite place to eat. We come here every year for my birthday but very rarely for afternoon tea or treats. Usually when we come Mom and I wear our galabya." Seeing the quizzical look on the twins' faces, Rana said, "Galabya are long, loose-fitting dresses. Egyptian women used to wear them all the time. I have a blue and gold one. They are beautiful and comfy. I'll have to show you mine when we go home."

As each item arrived, Rana gave her friends a lesson on Egyptian desserts and hospitality. First they took bites of *basbousa*, a traditional sweet cake made of cooked semolina and soaked in syrup. The restaurant's version had syrup made with orange flower water, which Samal thought was delicious. Next, they sampled *kunafa*, a sweet and crunchy dessert made with baked noodles and filled with mixed nuts and cream. The third treat was *Qara' Asali*. Anara thought it was like pumpkin pie without the crust.

Everything was going perfectly until a few minutes into the fourth course: *khushaf*. A mixture of apricots, prunes, raisins, almonds, pistachios, and pine nuts, the version at Kenooz Siwa was soaked in water flavored with rose water. Rana told the Nylunds that Muslims who are fasting during the holy month of Ramadan often eat this for breakfast before their day's fast begins.

Samal looked over at Ollie. His face was bright red, like he'd been running a race. "Ollie, what's wrong with you? You look funny!" Ollie's tongue was swollen and he couldn't talk.

"Oh my goodness!" Allison yelled. "I think he's having an allergic reaction to something in one of the desserts. Does Oliver have any food allergies?"

The twins shook their heads vigorously. "Not that we know of," they said.

Seeing their distress, the waiter quickly came over. "Leave the other kids here, ma'am. Get him to the clinic around the corner. Quick! Allah be with you."

By the time Allison grabbed Ollie, his face was starting to look like a pufferfish. His eyes were wild. He looked terrified. Rana and the twins sat at the table in silence for a bit. Then the waiter came back and brought a game of checkers. "He will be all right, girls. The doctors at that clinic are excellent. My son has allergies. Sometimes he has to get a shot to calm things down."

An hour later, Allison returned with a recovered Oliver. Both sisters hugged him. "Oh, Ollie – we were so worried about you. Are you okay now?"

"Yeah, I think so. The doctors think it was something in one of the desserts. They said I should get tested by an allergy doctor back home and try to avoid any nuts or spices I have not had before."

After they thanked the waiter many times, Rana asked if they could bring home a serving of *Umm Ali*, an Egyptian version of bread pudding, to Keb. Since there was no school the next day, Rana and her new friends watched a movie and played cards. After their scare at the restaurant, the kids were happy to have a quiet night in.

Chapter Five

Eid al-Adha celebrations

~~~~~~~~~~~~~~~~~~~~~~~~~~~~~~~~~~

When Rana woke up and walked into the kitchen, she found Ollie on the kitchen floor playing with some toy soldiers he'd brought from home. The twins were still snoozing.

"Morning, pumpkin. How'd you sleep?" Allison asked, ruffling Rana's black hair.

"Good, thanks. Are those muffins on the counter?"

"Yep, I baked them last night." Even if muffins weren't popular in Egypt, Allison still liked the taste of foods from back home. And, at this time of the year, she always baked late at night. Otherwise the apartment would feel like an inferno.

Keb had gotten up extra early and had a huge breakfast before the Sun was up. The day before Eid al-Adha was a fasting day for many Muslims so he needed to keep his strength up for the day ahead. After all, he wouldn't eat again until after dark. Rana was too young to have to fast yet.

"What is Eid al-Adha all about, Allison?" Oliver asked. "How come I saw so many sheep and cows in little fenced-in areas all over New Cairo?"

"You are a very bright young man, you know that?" Allison said. "Rana and I can tell you about the holiday while we walk, okay?"

Ollie looked up at her and smiled. "Yes, ma'am."

On the way to a farmers' market in New Cairo, Rana explained that Eid al-Adha is the Feast of the Sacrifice. This holiday marks the time of the Hajj, when millions of Muslims from around the world make a pilgrimage to the city of Mecca in Saudi Arabia. During this holiday, Muslims also remember the story of Abraham, who was ordered by God to sacrifice his son Ishmael. At the last moment in the story, God said he could slaughter an animal instead of his son.

Rana said Muslims around the world honored Abraham's faith by buying an animal to sacrifice. They then share the meat with their family and people in need. That's why Oliver noticed so many animals in pens. The twins were sad to hear that all those animals were going to be slaughtered.

At the market, Samal and Anara couldn't resist taking pictures of deep purple eggplants and jewel-like pomegranate seeds. Anara's name meant "pomegranate" in Kazakh. Her parents had met in Kazakhstan when they were in the Peace Corps.

The twins tried a refreshing glass of *karakadey*, a crimson drink made from hibiscus leaves. Oliver stuck to grape juice. Not far from the produce market was a stall that sold fireworks. Ollie couldn't believe it. "Wow! That's neat. You can't buy your own fireworks in New York for the Fourth of July," he announced.

"That's true, Ollie. But things are sometimes a bit different here. Fireworks are definitely a traditional part of our Eid celebrations in Egypt. I usually get sparklers and some small fireworks that Keb sets off. I think you'll have fun."

The strong Sun was wearing Oliver out. "Are there many more stops, Allison?"

"Nope. The last task for our Eid preparations is to get everyone a new outfit. Rana, why don't you tell our friends about the traditions?"

Rana said, "Everyone usually gets some new clothes for Eid al-Adha. Every year I choose a new colored galabya. Last year's was blue."

Anara and Samal figured that it would just be Allison and Rana getting new stuff, but there was still some leftover money from Mom. So, at a shop called Jumia, each girl picked a galabya. Rana's was orange with lime green embroidery. Samal picked a sky blue one with little silver beads at the top. And Anara opted for a lilac galabya with yellow details on the sleeves. Ollie snorted.

"Did you think we forgot you, Ollie?" Allison teased him. "Come with me and we'll get you a handsome looking galabya of your own." Anara and Samal weren't sure what their little brother would think of this idea. But he seemed thrilled to choose one with thin, dark blue stripes.

******

The next morning, the girls smelled something they didn't recognize. Rana said that during Eid al-Adha, people tended to eat a lot of meat. "Dad was up early to visit the butcher to have a sheep sacrificed for Eid al-Adha. He already brought home our family's third of the meat and is at the mosque now. So I think Mom's making sheep liver. That's what we always have for the holiday."

"Seriously?" Anara wrinkled her nose. "Sheep liver for breakfast? The smell is a bit much for me."

Rana looked offended. "It's really good. Mom is a great cook. Eating lots of meat as a celebration of the holiday is our tradition. I hope you'll try some."

The Nylunds looked at each other, then at the ground. None of them were keen to try liver.

"We probably will," Oliver mumbled. When Rana wasn't looking, Samal pinched Ollie's arm. There was no way she was eating liver for breakfast.

Later in the day, Oliver asked Keb what he was going to do with the rest of the sheep. Keb said he would take the rest of the meat to relatives, neighbors and the poor. The idea was that no one should be without meat on the table for Eid al-Adha.

"This is the first year in a long time that we aren't traveling during the holiday," Rana told them. "My grandparents are making the hajj so they are returning from Saudi Arabia. And my uncle's family lives in Alexandria. We'll visit them next year." Even though the holiday was different, Anara thought the patterns of visiting relatives were like Thanksgiving or Christmas back home.

Everyone put on their new clothes before boarding the bus to Keb's elderly aunt and uncle's home on the outskirts of Cairo. Earlier, the kids had helped make some rice pudding as a present. Samal thought that Aunt Heba and Uncle Mostafa were the cutest old couple. And Heba and Mostafa were thrilled to see so many young people in their home. Heba kept touching the twins' frizzy, light blond hair. And Mostafa couldn't get over that they were identical twins. Keb, Rana, and Allison all took turns translating because Heba and Mostafa only spoke Arabic. The eight of them sat in the living room and drank lots of very sweet *shai*, or tea.

Rana wanted to teach the guests how to play senet. Senet was thought to be the oldest board game in the world, played since the time of the pharaohs. Rana and Mostafa were skilled players.

They both gave Ollie and the girls good advice on how to play well. On his fifth game, Ollie beat Mostafa, though Mostafa may have helped him a little. Even though neither of them spoke the other's language, they had a great time.

After dark, Heba and Mostafa took everyone for a short walk up a nearby hill. Keb lit off some of the fireworks Allison bought. Some flared red and white. Another went really high and changed from pink to green. Everyone oohed and aahed, just like back in New York. Fireworks seemed to elicit the same enthusiasm from old and young people all over the world. Allison handed each child a sparkler to wave in celebration of a happy holiday. Finally, Keb set off some firecrackers as an end to the evening's festivities.

******

The next two days of Eid al-Adha were also eventful. One day the Nylunds ate at another of Rana's favorite restaurants. She introduced them to her favorite soup called *molokhia*. The soup was made of a leafy green vegetable, which people in the West call mallow. It was served with rice.

Oliver couldn't get enough of the hummus or the Egyptian flat bread called aish used to scoop it up.

After the meal, the kids went to see a movie about ancient Egypt. Samal thought it was great. "You'll see some of the things from this movie at the Egyptian Museum and when you travel with your mom," Rana told them. Oliver couldn't wait.

On the last day of Eid al-Adha, Allison and Keb took the kids to Dream Park, a super-cool amusement park. Samal, Allison, and Rana loved roller coasters, but Anara didn't. "Are you guys going to do crazy rides all day?" she asked, sounding annoyed. She gave Samal a fierce look. "You know I hate roller coasters. I don't want to spend all day with Ollie on the baby rides. He doesn't even meet the height requirement for half the rides."

Samal was not happy with Anara either. "You're being a grouch, Anara. It's your own fault that you don't like roller coasters. We're only going to be at Dream Park today and I don't want to miss all the cool stuff. Either be brave or stop whining."

Allison intervened. She wasn't used to sibling rivalry. Rana had her choice all the time. "Whoa, hold on a minute girls. Let's come up with a compromise. This is a special day for everybody. And the park is really crowded so I don't relish the idea of spending all day in long lines myself."

Ollie piped up, "Can't Anara spend part of the day with you and part with me and Keb?"

"Sounds like a plan," Keb replied. For the first half of the day, Samal, Rana, and Allison waited in lines and screamed on the crazy coasters. All the while Anara, Keb, and Ollie went on the bumper cars, the Crazy Pineapple, and the Dragon Boat. Later in the day, Rana joined her dad and Ollie while Allison and the twins browsed in the park's shops, did an old-fashioned photo shoot and played arcade games.

Just before bed, Ollie went into the kitchen. He said to Keb and Rana, "I wish we celebrated Eid al-Adha every year. The last few days have been awesome!"

Chapter Six

Exploring Cairo: Mummies and More

When Eid al-Adha ended, the kids were all pretty beat. After one mellow day at home, they headed to one of Rana's favorite places: Fagnoon Art School.

Anara, an art lover, was full of questions. "What's it like? Are there lessons? What media do people work in there? Are they strict about not making messes?" Mom was always giving Anara grief about the messes she made at home.

Rana answered, "You can take lessons but mostly it's pretty free form. People work in many kinds of media. Last time I was there, I made a glass necklace and a clay sculpture for my window."

"You mean that amazing mermaid sculpture in your room? You made that?" Samal asked. She couldn't believe that it wasn't store-bought.

Rana seemed embarrassed by the compliment. "I did," she said.

The Nylund kids loved that Fagnoon was located on 5 acres in the fields between Saqqara and Giza. Compared to Queens, Fagnoon felt like the middle of nowhere. The three girls wandered around and explored together while Allison kept Ollie company.

When they met up after an hour, Samal had already tried her hand at printmaking; Rana had sculpted another mermaid for her window; and Anara had made a beaded bracelet. Ollie was thrilled with the carpentry area. He couldn't wait to go back and create some more mini-buildings.

The excited crew spent almost the whole day at the art center, only breaking to have some *fiteer* for lunch. Fiteer was basically Egyptian pizza. The girls all wanted peppers, onions, tomatoes, and cheese as their fillings. The girls also tried dessert fiteer filled with powdered sugar, nuts, and dried coconut. After his allergy scare, Ollie ordered plain vanilla ice cream.

As the afternoon Sun began to dip, Oliver noticed that the Fagnoon Art School was in the shadow of what looked like a pyramid. He asked Allison if they could see it up close. As they approached, a guard came over and said that the tours of the complex were over for the day.

"Rats! I wish I knew this was here before. I wouldn't have made so many buildings. Now I'll never get to check out this cool pyramid." Oliver was very disappointed.

The guard said that the grounds would be open until dusk. The five of them spent about 45 minutes walking around Pharaoh Djoser's Step Pyramid. They looked at some of the courtyards and temples in the surrounding complex.

Samal read from a plaque: "This pyramid was originally designed to be a traditional flat-roofed mastaba, or tomb, but during the pharaoh's 19-year reign, it was built higher and higher. At the end of Pharaoh Djoser's reign, in 2611 BCE, the building stood 204 feet high."

Back at home, Ollie read online that it was the largest building of its time. And because the tomb was raided, all that was left of Pharaoh Djoser was his mummified left foot. The girls thought that was gross.

Rana said no visitor to Cairo should miss the Egyptian Museum. "It's amazing," she said. "I know you guys have all studied ancient Egypt so you have to see some of the treasures from that time. They're so cool!"

When the twins looked in their guidebook, they couldn't believe there were ten pages just on the museum's various floors, rooms, and galleries. That was more coverage than some entire cities got in the book!

Rana's high praise was not overestimated. But one thing irked Samal. Looking at the line that snaked around the building, she asked, "What's the holdup here? Even the line at the Metropolitan Museum of Art back home isn't this long!"

Rana said it normally took a while to go through security because, not long ago, vandals used tiny tools to damage some ancient statues. Now the security team checked everyone's bags thoroughly. Anara was sad that the security team made her throw out her bottle of pomegranate juice since no food or drink was allowed inside the museum.

Once they cleared the monstrous line,

everyone's moods improved. The six of them spent nearly the entire day wandering from room to room. Samal, Anara, and Oliver each had their favorite items on display. Samal loved the life-size pink granite sculpture of Hatshepsut, whom she thought was cool for having herself crowned as pharaoh. She also liked the unfinished head of Nefertiti, the wife of Akhenaten. It was made of brown quartzite. Samal thought it showed how beautiful Nefertiti really was.

Anara loved the blue faience hippopotamus from Egypt's Middle Kingdom. She found it interesting that the hippo was a symbol of how fertile the Nile River was. Being a bit of a jewelry fan, she also was delighted with the golden headband from Queen Sit-Hathor-Yunet. Dating from the 19th century BCE, it featured a rearing cobra with semiprecious stones.

Ollie was thrilled to see King Tut's death mask. It was made of solid gold and weighed more than 24 pounds. He'd seen pictures of it in a book but was thrilled to see it in person. Ollie also thought the sets of wooden warriors from the tomb of governor Mesehti were cool. These soldiers dated back to about 2000 BCE.

"Do you think anyone 4,000 years from now will find my collections of plastic toy soldiers?" he asked.

"You never know, Oliver, someone just might!" Keb replied.

When everyone felt like their brains were full, the group headed for a snack break. Keb led the way to Mandarine Koueider, a candy and dessert restaurant.

Rana wanted some homemade pistachio ice cream and a couple of chocolate covered dates, but the Nylund kids couldn't decide. They'd never heard of most of the things on the menu.

Keb spoke up. "I'll choose a bunch of things for you to try. If you don't like something, it's okay. I like everything." He grinned and rubbed his belly. At that moment, Keb reminded Samal of a statue of Buddha she'd seen in New York.

Oliver stuck to a simple-but-safe rice pudding dish. The twins enjoyed *arameesh*, or candied pistachios, and *kahk*, sugar cookies filled with mixed dates and nuts. When Anara said she'd like to learn to make kahk, Keb said he'd happily share his grandma's recipe with her.

Heading out from Mandarine Koueider, Samal thought Cairo's air looked brown and gritty. It definitely wasn't the cleanest city she'd ever seen. But little did any of them know that pollution was

wrong place, wrong time

about to become the least of their worries.

Before heading back to New Cairo, Samal, Anara, and Oliver wanted to see a few famous landmarks near the Egyptian Museum. The area was crowded as always. Out of the corner of her eye, Anara saw a group of people holding signs across Tahrir Square. She didn't think much of it, though she did notice that Allison and Keb gave each other a strange look. Dozens of people were protesting against the Egyptian government. Some held signs. Others were banging on pots and pans or setting off firecrackers.

As they walked past the Metro station, a loud bang seemed to come from nowhere. Oliver let out a squeal. His pupils were huge. Keb was mad. He approached one of the men making the racket. "Could you stop that noise, please? You're

frightening the children."

The guy began yelling about his right to say whatever he wanted, as loudly as he wanted. Then he shoved Keb.

"Dad, let's go! Dad, come on!" Rana insisted. Allison tried to get Keb and the kids away from the scene. She'd seen enough political demonstrations in Tahrir Square on TV. They didn't always end well.

A pack of police headed in their direction. These weren't just the crossing guard types of police that the twins saw every morning near their school in Queens. They were riot police dressed in battle gear with sticks and gas masks. One of the policemen approached Keb. Allison's face went white. Clearly, the police thought that Keb was part of the problem. She tried to get closer to the police to explain what was going on, but they blocked off the area and would not let her come nearer.

A few minutes later, Keb was handcuffed and pushed into the back of a squad car. Then, he was gone.

Rana and Allison were crying. As they made

their way toward the station, the protestors who were holding the signs started throwing rocks at the police. The police shot rubber bullets into the crowd. The square quickly cleared out. Anara, Samal, and Oliver stayed quiet. None of them knew what to do or say.

They waited for two hours at the bus station. Keb didn't show up. Allison kept calling his cell phone, with no luck. Finally, they went back to their apartment in New Cairo. Rana looked out her bedroom window and sobbed. Allison called every Cairo police station she could find the phone number for. But no one had any information about Keb.

Anara and Samal weren't trying to eavesdrop but Allison's voice was loud on the phone. She finally called Mom. The twins heard just bits and pieces of the conversation: "Keb was taken by the police ... He's been gone for five hours ... No one at the station will tell me anything ... What if they put him in jail, or worse? ... What am I going to do, Jess? I have to find out what's happened. It's driving me crazy."

It took everyone a long time to fall asleep that night. Luckily Mom was already scheduled to come back the following day.

When Oliver woke up the next morning, he found Allison asleep at the kitchen table. Allison stirred when she felt Ollie's hand touch hers. "It will be okay, Allison. Keb didn't do anything wrong. He'll be back soon."

Allison's eyes filled with tears. "Thank you, Oliver. I hope you are right."

Rana turned on the TV. There was a report on the morning news about what happened in Tahrir Square. The antigovernment protestors had broken car windows, blocked off a couple of major roads, and burned tires near the square. More than 200 police were called in to stop the demonstration. The TV reporter explained that the protestors had not gotten permission from the Ministry of the Interior for their protest and were violating Egyptian law. Several people were sent to local hospitals with injuries.

About an hour after they watched the news, there was a knock on the door. It was Keb! Rana and Allison hugged him tightly and didn't let go. Keb's eyes were bloodshot and his hair was a bit messy, but otherwise he looked okay. Keb said he wanted to take a shower and that he would tell everybody what happened when he got out.

The kids all squeezed in on the living room couch while Keb and Allison snuggled up on the loveseat. He explained that he was brought to the central police station and had to wait in handcuffs for hours before anyone checked in with him. Then some detectives had brought him into an interrogation room. They asked him all kinds of questions about why he was in Tahrir Square and how he knew the demonstrators. The police also checked Keb's records to see if he had any history of being involved in demonstrations. He didn't. By the time the police finished with him, it was nearly dawn but still too early for the buses to be running to New Cairo.

Keb apologized for all the drama. The Nylunds couldn't wait for Mom to get back.

Chapter Eight

Pyramids, Camel Rides, and Markets

~~~~~~~~~~~~~~~~~~~~~~~~~~~~~~~~~

The kids were watching a movie when the apartment buzzer sounded. Oliver ran to the door and opened it.

"Mom!" He jumped into her arms. The twins rushed to hug her, too.

On their last night together, Rana and Ollie made a fort out of blankets in the living room and played backgammon. The twins helped cook a big dinner of Egyptian foods and chocolate cake for dessert.

Just before heading out the next morning, Rana took some pictures of Anara, Samal, and Oliver out on the apartment's balcony. The morning Sun cast a beautiful glow on the city.

Then they said their goodbyes.

******

The Nylunds spent a day hanging out at their

Cairo hotel's rooftop swimming pool before their busy week of family adventures began. Samal was the queen of cannonballs. Anara could hold an underwater handstand for 43 seconds. And Ollie splashed more than anyone thought was possible.

During a little break, Ollie sat under the shade of a big umbrella sipping *qasab*, sugarcane juice. Sugarcane was planted all over southern Egypt because the soils and temperatures were perfect for it. The juice was a pale green color. Samal drank guava blended with milk. She loved experimenting with tropical fruits, from dragon fruit to papaya. Anara sometimes chose her beverages based on their color. On the pool deck, she chose the crimson-colored hibiscus juice known as Karakadey.

When the tour bus rolled up early the next morning, Oliver couldn't wait to get going. They were heading to see pyramids and the Sphinx! The bus stopped at a couple of other hotels to get passengers before heading onto the highway. The last stop for pickup was the Mena House Hotel. Samal, the architecture fan, nearly went crazy when she saw it. Its palm trees, palace-like design and view of the Pyramids were outrageous. Even though she couldn't draw as well as Anara, she made a quick sketch in her journal to document the Mena House. And she told Mom, "If we ever come back to Cairo, let's stay here for a night."

"Sounds like a plan, lovebug. It does look amazing. Put it in your memory banks for the future."

Samal pointed to her head and smirked. "I already have," she replied.

As the bus got closer to Giza, Anara thought it was weird to have parking lots in the middle of the desert. She thought it was such a contrast to the camels, which must have taken early tourists to the site.

Their guide, Ahmed, spoke perfect English. He led them up a steep, crude set of stairs at the Great Pyramid of Khufu. Ollie, Samal, and Mom climbed the rickety stairs with no trouble. But Anara had never been a big fan of heights. She made it up the first few steps. Then she looked down.

"I can't do this," she announced. "It's too high. This staircase is scary. You guys go without me."

Beads of sweat covered Anara's forehead. Her face turned a pale shade of green.

Ahmed remained calm. "You can do this. I know you can." He descended the staircase until he was two rungs above Anara. "I'm going to tie two cords between your belt and mine. They will keep you from falling. Just watch the cords as you climb up. I'll be attached to you the whole time."

Anara gulped. "I don't know, Ahmed. I hate these tiny rungs. I feel like I'm going to fall down into a pit." She noticed a group of tourists waiting below her, watching to see what would happen next. "These people are rushing me," she said.

"No, no. Let's just give it a try. If you really can't get up there, I can leave you with my colleagues down below. But I would hate for you to miss this chance to see the amazing treasures inside this pyramid." Ahmed's voice was confident and soothing.

Anara climbed. After a couple of minutes, she reached the top of the stairs. Her shirt was soaked in sweat. "Thank you, Ahmed. I'm sorry."

"It's okay, dear. These things happen. Every now

and then I have to help someone on this ladder. We all need help sometimes, yes?" He patted her back. Finally, they were able to enter some small shafts and eventually go into a burial room made entirely of granite. Oliver said he felt like Indiana Jones. Even Anara agreed.

Climbing through the ancient structure was slightly scary because some passages were low and narrow. As they walked through the Great Gallery, Ahmed told them to notice how precisely the blocks in the ceiling all fit together. Oliver liked the red granite blocks that made up the walls of the King's Chamber. After the frightening climb, Anara was grateful for the air flowing inside the pyramid. A modern ventilation system was built into the pyramid's ancient airshafts.

When they got back outside, Ahmed showed them three small structures that looked like pyramid-shaped rubble piles. These were the tombs of the pharaoh Khufu's wives and sisters.

Samal was surprised to learn that Khufu began construction of the Great Pyramid almost as soon as he took the throne in the 26th century BCE.

He was only in his twenties at the time so she wondered why he was already thinking about a burial place. But the project took about 23 years to complete. Oliver remarked he still couldn't quite understand how these early builders managed to move 2,300,000 blocks of stone. Particularly since each one weighed about two and a half tons.

"That would not have been the job for me," Samal said. "I can barely carry a heavy grocery bag up to our apartment."

Ahmed laughed. "True enough. Not to mention the blazing Sun beating down on the workers. Probably no lunch breaks with thermoses of lemonade either."

After Ahmed finished his tour of the Giza pyramids, he led the group on a walk toward the Sphinx. Everyone started whipping out their cameras. Samal said this had to be the ultimate shot of ancient Egyptian landmarks with the Sphinx in front and the pyramids in the background. Even though some people in their group said the Sphinx looked smaller in person than in books or on TV, the Nylund kids were still impressed.

Anara liked the fact that the Sphinx was known in Arabic as *Abu al-Hol*, which means "Father of Terror." She also appreciated that each of its paws was longer than a city bus. Apparently the nose of this part-cat, part-man statue was hammered off between the 11th and 15th centuries. Oliver thought it was hilarious that part of the Sphinx's beard was on display at the British Museum in London. He kept joking about where the other part might be. Samal was impressed that the huge sculpture was made from a single piece of limestone. They savored the view, and some fresh juice, on the outdoor terrace just below the Sphinx.

Chapter Nine

In the Footsteps of Greatness

All three kids loved the evening on the sleeper train to Aswan. Mom and Oliver took one cabin and the twins shared their own cabin next door. Within an hour of boarding the train, the staff delivered their dinner. The food reminded Samal of the frozen dinner in a metal tray she'd had once at a friend's house: chicken, a roll, and slightly mushy vegetables. Ollie said it was like astronaut trays. Later, porters came to fold down the beds. Anara loved the beds' coziness. The click-clack of the tracks and slightly lilting motion had the four of them asleep in a flash.

The girls woke up early the next morning. Unsure of whether Mom and Ollie were still sleeping, they decided to slip out of their cabin to scope out the dining car. Samal was impressed by its fancy dark wood and green leather seats. They watched people sipping cups of tea and coffee.

When Ollie knocked on the girls' cabin door, he got no response. "Mom," he said, "they didn't answer."

"They must be really sleeping. I'll just leave them a note and we'll get breakfast." When Ollie turned the key in their cabin door, he found the beds empty.

Mom was furious. She headed to the dining car. It didn't take long for her to find the twins. "You are not supposed to just wander around, girls. What if someone took you off the train? You could have been in Al Qasr by now, for all I'd know. Do not do that again without talking to me first. Am I clear?"

"Why are you so mad?" Samal asked. "It's not like we could go anywhere far." The girls were both surprised at Mom's reaction. They thought it was kind of like being on a plane where people just walked around to pass the time.

"Well, a train does have stops, you know. It's not quite as enclosed as an airplane. I just worry, that's all. Tourists do get kidnapped sometimes."

After the angst passed, the four of them enjoyed a simple breakfast: rolls with butter and jam and tea. The views from the dining car's window were spectacular. Ollie and his sisters saw men and women weeding, planting, and carrying baskets of crops in the fields along the Nile River. Samal guessed some were sugarcane fields and that others were for cotton. Egypt was famous for its soft, good-quality cotton. She knew that because Dad loved Egyptian cotton sheets.

More than 13 hours after they departed Cairo, the Nylunds arrived at Aswan station. They all felt a bit grungy. The sleeper cabins only had little sinks for washing up. Quick showers at their new hotel boosted everyone's spirits.

Walking down toward the Nile River, Anara said, "I can't believe how wide the river is here. It's ginormous! Are those islands in the middle?"

"You bet. Aswan is a great city. And sunset is the perfect time to see the river up close. I was thinking of taking a felucca ride on the river. You guys up for that?"

"What's a felucca?" Ollie asked.

"It's an Egyptian sailing boat. They've been around for eons," Samal told him.

Mom was impressed. "Well done, Samal! The guides here in Aswan tend to be Nubian. Nubia is an ancient region in southern Egypt and northern Sudan. Today the Nubian people are a minority in Egypt but they take great pride in their culture. Part of the reason I had you girls wear longer skirts here is to be respectful of their beliefs."

After checking out the various felucca operators, they found one that had space for everyone. Anara bought some bottled water from a vendor before boarding the boat. Allison had said it was a bad idea to drink any un-bottled water since it could give you stomach troubles. Ollie preferred the word "diarrhea."

The felucca traveled pretty slowly. Samal thought it was like stepping back in time a little. Offshore, they sailed past islands studded with palm trees. Anara noticed black granite boulders in the waters. Their first stop was a little island called Kitchener's Island. For about 30 minutes,

Ollie ran along the Aswan Botanical Gardens' paths pretending to be an explorer. Anara sketched her favorite plants and palm trees. Samal and Mom chatted about what life must have been like here thousands of years ago.

Back on the boat, the felucca guide Mohamed headed to Elephantine Island. They visited Siou and Koti, two of the island's Nubian villages. Mohamed led everyone on a peaceful walk down shady alleys and by little gardens. The group stopped in for tea at Baaba Dool, a brightly painted Nubian house.

Ollie was excited about some tiny lizards he saw scurrying by. But Samal and Anara were more thrilled about the henna tattoos they saw advertised. Some local women came out from their homes and created tattoos for several people in their group. Samal asked for a cat on her right shoulder. Anara wanted a painter's palette on her left calf. And Ollie, not wanting to miss out, decided on a triangular pattern around his upper arm. The tattoo artists said the designs would last about two weeks, long enough to show their friends back home. Anara took some photos on Mom's cell phone and emailed them to Dad.

On the morning of their second day in Aswan, the Nylunds went bird-watching. They rented binoculars to see how many species they could identify. In the first half hour, Anara discovered the Nile Valley Sunbird, Whiskered Tern, Common Bulbul, and the Olivaceous Warbler. But after an hour or so, Oliver had a hard time keeping quiet. He darted down various paths, making screeching noises and imitating other birds he'd heard. Mom had to keep shushing him.

Eventually, a couple decked out with super-fancy cameras and gear approached them. "We paid a lot of money to come see the birds here." Glaring at Oliver, the woman continued, "You are really disrupting the birds' activity. Perhaps you could run around somewhere else." A couple of other seriously birdwatchers stood behind the disgruntled lady, nodding their heads in agreement.

Ollie looked like he might cry. Mom told the couple that she thought bird-watching was a family friendly activity and that she too had paid to come here. Still, a little while later, the Nylunds bailed out on the birds.

After the morning's embarrassment, they headed to Aswan's big market: Sharia as-Souq. At least it was a louder venue, Samal decided. Local people shopped for fruits, veggies, and live animals to bring home for dinner. When Anara asked why pigeons were for sale, she was surprised to learn that people throughout Egypt commonly ate them. "Really? At home people call pigeons 'flying rats.' That is not inspiring when you think of eating them for dinner."

Samal said, "One man's fried chicken is another man's baked pigeon. I guess it's partly what you grow up with." As they passed a stand selling camel meat, she said, "Camel meat! Ew! It may be local but it's not appealing."

When they were out of earshot of the camel meat stall, Mom whispered, "It's not really my thing either, to be honest."

Samal stopped to look at the perfume vendors and the stalls selling colorful Nubian baskets. The scent of sandalwood made the market seem exotic.

At the end of their day in Aswan, the foursome headed to Luxor. "Train, bus, taxi, I'm sick of moving around," Anara complained.

"I know, love, but I want you to see as much as you can. Chin up – we'll be staying in the same hotel in Luxor for the next three days." Oliver was also crabby, so the twins were grateful when he fell asleep on the ride. They all appreciated the air conditioning.

Luckily, Oliver and his sisters were full of pep when they woke up the next morning. On their first morning in Luxor, they rode in a small van to the Valley of the Kings.

"Could you guys call me Dr. Nylund? I want to be an archaeologist today," Ollie said.

Samal rolled her eyes and said, "Yes, sir." She had a bit less patience with Ollie's imagination games than Anara. But Mom shot Samal a look that meant business.

The early morning light made everything in the Valley look almost golden. Samal thought it was eerie. Their tour guide was an Egyptian woman named Deena. She told the group that she'd studied archaeology at Cairo University.

Deena started the tour with a brief overview of what they'd see in the Valley of the Kings. "This whole complex contains 63 royal tombs from the New Kingdom period, between 1550 and 1069 BCE. These tombs are all quite different from one another. Almost all of the pharaohs from Tuthmosis I to Ramesses XI decided to be buried in tombs in the Valley of the Kings. Why, you might ask, was this such a great burial spot? Well, for one thing, the narrow entrance to the valley was easy to guard. Some tombs were even hidden high in the cliffs."

"What about the Hall of Gold?" Ollie asked.

"Wow – great question! This was where a king was buried, along with jewelry, fancy furniture, royal clothing and other treasures. You've probably all heard or read about the tomb of King Tutankhamun. His was the only tomb in the Valley of the Kings that was practically left untouched by robbers. Let's go explore. Feel free to ask questions as we go through the Valley."

Oliver took Deena's statement to heart. Between her tour stops, he peppered her with questions about being an archaeologist, sites she'd visited, and proper digging techniques. She seemed flattered that someone was so interested in her work. They spent just about the entire day poring over the treasures. Everyone's favorite was King Tut's tomb. All three kids couldn't resist getting a few cheesy souvenirs – pyramid-shaped key chains, a snow globe with the Sphinx inside, and a Halloween-style mask of King Tut's golden death mask.

By late afternoon, everyone was sweaty and worn out. Anara had to share a fact she'd read in her guidebook: "Did you know that the average visitor to the Valley leaves behind 2.8 grams of sweat and that it's having a negative effect on the reliefs and the wall paintings here?"

"Ew! That's so gross!" Samal said. "But I think Ollie has exceeded that sweat average. Look at his hair – it's sopping wet!" Mom told Samal to chill out and leave Dr. Nylund alone. She also said there was one last surprise for the day.

Chapter Ten

Camels, underwater Frights, and اعداً (Goodbye), Egypt

"What's the big surprise, Mom?" Ollie asked.

"We're going on a camel ride!" she said.

"No way!" Anara shrieked. Samal's eyes got huge and Ollie bounced up and down in his seat.

"Yes way," Mom replied. "I thought it would be cool to see a little of the desert the old-fashioned way." Their leader, Sherif, helped the Nylunds get onto their kneeling camels. They wore blankets and saddles on their furry backs. When the camels stood up, Sherif said to hold on tight or they might feel wobbly. Samal thought it was crazy and exciting to be ten feet up in the air while riding a loping beast.

For two hours, they trekked from Luxor's West Bank through some green fields, farmland, and local villages. Anara loved the view of the desert. But every time her camel bent down to munch some vegetation, she got nervous. And for good reason: In the middle of the walk, a snake slithered across the path they were on.

"You guys! I think that's a viper! What if my camel drops me? Oh, I hate snakes!" Anara shrieked. Samal screamed like a horror film star. The camels did not seem too happy either, with hysterical humans on their backs.

Sherif quickly took control of the situation. "Relax, my friends. This is a harmless African egg-eating snake. It wants nothing to do with us."

Anara felt like her heart was beating in her throat. Samal held her camel's reins so tightly that her hands turned bright red. Sherif reminded them to enjoy the spectacular sunset view of Luxor. His wife served them mint tea after they dismounted from their camels.

Just before leaving Luxor, Ollie and his sisters enjoyed the nighttime sound-and-light show at Karnak. As they walked through the complex of temples, pharaohs appeared to tell their life stories. Music played and colored lights threw cool shadows on the buildings and statues. Ollie loved when voices seemed to pop out of nowhere. One told about the birth of Karnak temple, back in the reign of King Seti I. Samal thought the experience was a little cheesy but admitted it was also kind of fun to see everything lit up at night.

Between going to school, celebrating holidays, and moving around, the trip to Egypt had been intense. The kids wanted to end the trip with some fun in the Sun. So they spent their last two nights in Egypt in the town of Hurghada. Despite their fair hair and serious need for sunscreen, the twins were total beach bums. They swam for hours in the hotel's huge pool. Then they splashed in the shallows of the Red Sea.

On their very last day, they went snorkeling to see the coral reefs and marine life. Oliver wasn't a strong enough swimmer to snorkel out in the open sea so he stayed on the glass-bottomed boat. The twins decided to try snorkeling with an instructor. Anara was checking out the lionfish, stingrays, and angelfish when she noticed Samal flailing about. She'd swallowed a snorkel full of water and was starting to panic.

"Help! Help! My sister's in trouble!" Anara cried when she saw Samal thrashing. The instructor swam quickly and pulled Samal back to the boat. Her face was green. As soon as she got on deck, she threw up everywhere. Besides being completely humiliated, Samal felt sick to her stomach. Mom rubbed her back for the next two hours. Anara lost her desire to go back in the water. They all just sat around the glass-bottomed part of the boat watching whatever came by. They saw an eel and lots of neon-colored fish.

Over dinner that night, Samal apologized. "I'm sorry if I ruined everyone's day on the boat. I guess I'm not as strong a swimmer as I thought I was." She looked down at the table.

"That's okay," Ollie said. "I liked everyone looking through the glass with me. Maybe you can take swimming lessons with me this winter."

Samal scoffed at the idea of lessons. They dropped the subject and looked out over the turquoise waters while eating at the hotel's outdoor restaurant. Even with her rough day, Samal hadn't lost her sense of humor. "Don't you guys think it's weird that the Red Sea is actually turquoise?"

"I noticed that too," Anara commented. "They should have given it a more fitting title, like aqua or cerulean."

"Only you, Ms. Artsy, would even know the word cerulean," Samal quipped. They all enjoyed their meals, a mixture of Egyptian and Italian food. Anara thought the baba ghanouj, or eggplant spread, was the best she'd ever had. And the pomegranate ice cream was to die for, in Samal's opinion.

Just after boarding the plane from Cairo to New York, Mom asked the kids to write one more time in their journals before they forgot anything. She also wanted to know how they thought the trip went overall.

"I hope the next time you get a last-minute assignment, Dad has a conference. This was awesome!" Ollie said.

Anara's travel journal

I'm on the bus back from Hurghada, making my way to Cairo International Airport. This trip to Egypt has been incredible! Allison and Keb gave me Egyptian cooking lessons. Here's Keb's kahk recipe:

Ingredients:
2 cups semolina flour
1 1/2 cups shortening
1 cup boiling water
1/2 teaspoon salt
3/4 cup white sugar
1 teaspoon cinnamon
2 cups ground walnuts
1/4 cup confectioners' sugar
2 teaspoons orange blossom water

Directions:

1. Place the semolina flour and salt into a medium bowl, and mix in shortening using a fork.

2. Pour in a cup of boiling water, and mix to form a solid dough. Let cool for a couple of minutes then turn the dough onto a lightly floured surface. Knead for a minute or two to be sure the dough is well-blended.

3. Cover the dough and let stand for at least one hour, but not longer than overnight.

4. Preheat the oven to 350 degrees. Be sure to grease the cookie sheets.

5. In a medium bowl, mix together the white sugar, ground walnuts, cinnamon and orange blossom water. Make sure the mixture is thoroughly combined. Set aside.

6. Knead dough again briefly, and form into walnut-sized balls. Make a hole in the center using your finger. Fill the hole with the nut mixture, and seal the dough up over it.

7. Place cookies at least an inch apart onto the prepared cookie sheets.

8. Bake for 10 to 12 minutes or until lightly browned. Dust with confectioners' sugar while still hot.

Fun Facts About Egypt

Capital: Cairo

Official Language: Arabic

Population: 89,895,099 (July 2014 estimate)

Famous People: Cleopatra VII (c.69 BCE-30 BCE), Tutankhamun (c. 1344 BCE – 1327 BCE), Anwar Sadat (1918-1981)

Holidays Celebrated: National Day (July 23); Many Egyptians also celebrate Islamic holidays such as Eid al-Adha, also called Feast of the Sacrifice

Climate: hot, dry summers and moderate winters; very little rainfall

Significant Events:

c. 2500 BCE – Egyptians build the Great Pyramid of Giza.

c. 640 CE – Egypt becomes part of the Islamic Empire.

1517 – Ottoman Empire invades Egypt, beginning a 300-year reign.

1869 – Suez Canal, which connects the Red Sea with the Mediterranean Sea, is completed.

1922 – Egypt gains limited independence from Britain; King Tut's tomb is discovered.

1953 – Egypt is declared a republic.

1978 – President Anwar Sadat signs peace agreement with Israel.

2011 – Hosni Mubarak resigns from his role as President of Egypt.

The porter on our overnight train from Cairo to Aswan gave me a map of Egypt because it showed places we visited like Karnak, Luxor, and Hurghada. I wanted to keep it as a souvenir. It's pretty cool!

Here are a few of the fish we saw through the glass-bottomed boat on the Red Sea:

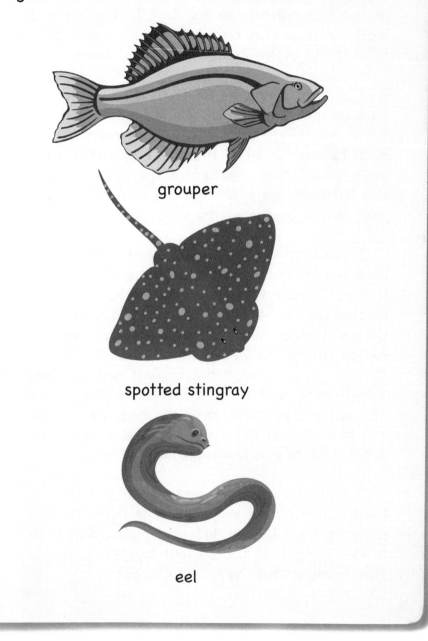

grouper

spotted stingray

eel

Wandering through some of the tombs in the Valley of the Kings was one of the best parts of the trip. Getting to see King Tut's gold death mask up close was crazy! I bought a postcard of it to put on my bulletin board at home.

I think it would be amazing if we could go back in time and see what the landscape of Egypt was like when the pharaohs ruled. It's hard to imagine what the Valley of the Kings must have looked like before the Sphinx and the Pyramids were there. All I can picture is just desert as far as the eye could see.

I was hoping to see the city of Alexandria on this trip, but there wasn't time. Alexandria is Egypt's second largest city after Cairo. It's located on the Mediterranean Sea. Queen Cleopatra made her throne here. I wanted to see where the Great Library was located. Scholars from around the ancient world visited that library in their hunt for knowledge. Many of the library's treasures have been destroyed, but the city opened a beautiful new library in 2002. It's shaped like a discus.

I sketched and took pictures of some of my favorite plants and animals in Egypt. The papyrus plant looked different than I'd pictured it. It's funny that the ancient Egyptians used this to make their version of paper:

Since I know I'll never see a hoopoe at my birdfeeder in Queens, I captured it on Mom's iPhone:

These hoopoe birds are even depicted on some ancient Egyptian artworks.

Discussion Questions:

1. How is life in Egypt today similar to your own life? How is it different?

2. With such a dry climate, how do you think the Egyptians managed to grow crops and develop such an advanced civilization?

3. If you could talk to any historical figure from Egypt's past, who would it be and what would you like to ask him or her?

4. How has Egyptian life changed from the days of the pharaohs to today?

5. If you had the chance to travel to Egypt, where would you most want to visit and why?

6. Compare the food that people eat in Egypt to the food you eat at home.

Vocabulary Words:

archaeologist	mosque
demonstrators	outskirts
elicit	passport
expedited	Peace Corps
frenzy	pilgrimage
inferno	quip
irrigation	quizzical
lilting	sacrifice
loping	ventilation

Ways to learn these new words:

- Make flash cards with the word on one side and the definition on the other side.
- Use one of these words in a sentence.
- Draw a picture to represent the meaning of a word.
- Write a story using some of the vocabulary words.

Learn more about Egypt, its landmarks and traditions:

timeforkids.com/destination/egypt

kids.nationalgeographic.com/explore/countries/egypt/

scholastic.com/teachers/article/fast-facts-egypt

About the Author:

Alicia Klepeis began her career at the National Geographic Society. In addition to her picture book *Francisco's Kites*, she is also the author of *Africa* and *Understanding Saudi Arabia Today*. Alicia loves to research fun and out-of-the-ordinary topics that make nonfiction exciting for readers. Her most recent titles include *The World's Strangest Foods*, *Bizarre Things We've Called Medicine*, and *Vampires: The Truth Behind History's Creepiest Bloodsuckers*. Alicia is currently working on a middle-grade novel, as well as several projects involving international food, American history, and world cultures. She lives with her family in upstate New York.

About the Illustrator:

Simon Abbott has
been illustrating
children's books
for 15 years. He
specializes in

bold colors and delightful characters of all kinds
and describes his work as fun, fresh and happy.
His easy style has instant appeal and helps to
communicate complex ideas and concepts in
an instant. Whether he is drawing playground
fun, astronauts, dinosaurs or monkeys swinging
through trees, his art is always engaging and is
guaranteed to make children smile. Simon lives
and works in Suffolk, England, with his partner
Sally, and 3 boys called Jack, Nathan and Alfie.